AF228573

Law Enforcement

K9

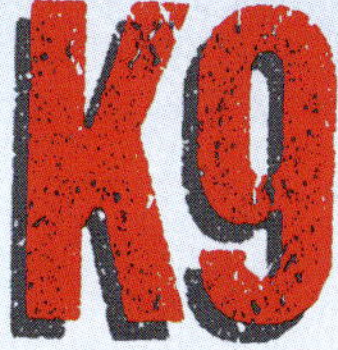

Abdo & Daughters

An imprint of Abdo Publishing | abdobooks.com

John Hamilton

ABDOBOOKS.COM

Published by Abdo Publishing, a division of ABDO, PO Box 398166, Minneapolis, Minnesota 55439. Copyright © 2022 by Abdo Consulting Group, Inc. International copyrights reserved in all countries. No part of this book may be reproduced in any form without written permission from the publisher. Abdo & Daughters™ is a trademark and logo of Abdo Publishing.

Printed in the United States of America, North Mankato, Minnesota.
102021
012022

Editor: Sue Hamilton
Copy Editor: Bridget O'Brien
Graphic Design: Sue Hamilton
Cover Design: Victoria Bates
Cover Photo: iStock
Interior Images: AP-pgs 4, 7, 16, 30, 36 & 45; Getty-pg 41; Eden Prairie Police Department-pg 39; iStock-pgs 6, 8, 14, 17, 20, 23, 34, 35 & 44; Library of Congress-pg 13; Lower Merion Township Police-pg 32 (bottom); Riverside County Sheriff's Department-pg 43; Shutterstock-pgs 1, 5, 9, 18, 19, 21, 22, 24, 25,27, 29, 31, 32 (top), 37, 38 & 40; Warrington Police K9 Unit-pgs 15, 28 & 33 (top); Wikimedia-pg 10.

LIBRARY OF CONGRESS CONTROL NUMBER: 2019956066

PUBLISHER'S CATALOGING-IN-PUBLICATION DATA

Names: Hamilton, John, author.

Title: K9 / by John Hamilton

Description: Minneapolis, Minnesota : Abdo Publishing, 2022 | Series: Law Enforcement | Includes online resources and index

Identifiers: ISBN 9781532193866 (lib. bdg.) | ISBN 9781644945841 (pbk.) | ISBN 9781098212643 (ebook)

Subjects: LCSH: Law enforcement--Juvenile literature. | Police dogs--Juvenile literature. | Animals in police work--Juvenile literature. | Police--Juvenile literature.

Classification: DDC 363.2--dc23

TABLE OF CONTENTS

K9 ON PATROL

In modern law enforcement, trained dogs are called K9s. This comes from the word *canine*, which comes from the Latin word for dog—*canis*. Police dogs give their human partners a huge advantage in dangerous situations. They are loyal, fearless, and they never quit. Police K9s use their incredible noses to find drugs and bombs, or to track criminals and hold them until human officers arrive to make an arrest.

Most major-city police departments use K9 units. Thousands of these loyal, highly trained dogs work on the streets every day. Much is asked of them. Some have even given their lives to protect and serve their human partners as well as the public.

A New York City cop and his K9 partner guard an area as people arrive for a Macy's Thanksgiving Day parade.

A police K9 and
its human handler
work as a team,
often patrolling
city streets.

K9s are used by many kinds of law enforcement agencies.

What is a police dog?

Put simply, police dogs are tools used by law enforcement officers. But K9s are so much more than that. They are a lifeline when cops are in danger. They are natural-born protectors who will give their own lives without question. When given a task, they never quit. They are so important to law enforcement that they are considered police officers, just like their human partners.

Police dogs can do many things that human cops can't do as well. They are fast, running between 35 and 38 miles per hour (56 to 61 kph). By comparison, the fastest human on the planet, Olympic champion Usain Bolt, once ran a race at a top speed of about 28 miles per hour (45 kph). When many criminals see a "fur missile" speeding toward them, they simply give up.

Not only are police dogs much faster than people, their noses are thousands of times more sensitive. Police departments around the country use K9 officers to search buildings, track fleeing criminals, and sniff out illegal items such as drugs or bombs. They can also find narcotics or weapons dropped by suspects during chases.

A Texas K9 team checks for drugs in a vehicle.

A K9 sniffs for hidden drugs or explosives in a suitcase.

Single-purpose or dual-purpose dogs

Police dogs are eager to please their handlers. They are also determined to win whenever they fight criminals. Some police dogs are single-purpose K9 units. That means they have one job, usually helping a patrol officer track down and apprehend suspects. Other dogs are dual purpose. In addition to regular patrol duties, they also sniff out hidden drugs or explosives.

Are police dogs mean?

It is a myth that police dogs are mean. They have an important job, and that's what they've been trained to do since they were puppies. Just as there are mean poodles, there are some mean police dogs. But most K9 dogs are fun loving. Doing their job is like play to them. If they perform correctly, they get praise or a favorite toy.

CAN I PET HIM?

When most people see a K9 working, they want to approach and pet the dog. That is rarely allowed. The dogs are on duty. They are not pets and should not be touched. It is work time for them, not social time. Also, many of the dogs do not like to be handled by strangers. It is important to first ask the handler if it is okay to touch the dog. The officer will say why it's okay, or not okay, to pet the dog. In general, cops prefer that people do not touch their dogs. They're doing a job and shouldn't be distracted.

Chapter 2

HISTORY OF POLICE DOGS

Dogs are the descendants of gray wolves. Humans domesticated them thousands of years ago. They helped track and hunt prey animals such as deer, and were also used as guard dogs.

Dog breeds as we know them today have only been around for the past few centuries. People have bred dogs to enhance certain behaviors and physical traits. Today, there are hundreds of breeds. Each has its own strengths and weaknesses.

A thief tries unsuccessfully to bribe a guard dog with food in an illustration from the 1600s.

Kublai Khan hunts with some of his 5,000 dogs. He holds the record for owning the most dogs by a single person.

Certain dogs have been trained for use in war and law enforcement since the Middle Ages. Kublai Khan was the grandson of Genghis Khan, and the fifth Khagan, or emperor, of the Mongol Empire. He owned more than 5,000 dogs, according to Venetian explorer and writer Marco Polo. Most of the dogs were Tibetan mastiffs, a strong, massive breed that Kublai Khan used for warfare and hunting. They have a bite strength that exceeds 550 pounds (249 kg) per square inch, similar to a lion's bite.

European and Asian law enforcement officers used dogs for protection against criminals. Scottish slough dogs, similar to today's bloodhounds, were used to track fugitives. They came to be known as sleuth hounds, or thief catchers.

London bobbies follow bloodhounds Burgho and Barnaby as they prove they can track Jack the Ripper.

Police dogs in Europe in the 1800s and 1900s

In the late 1800s, the notorious serial killer Jack the Ripper terrorized London, England. In 1888, the English police enlisted the help of a pair of bloodhounds to track him down. Although the wily murderer was never caught, the use of police dogs was increasing all over Europe.

London police, called bobbies, were sometimes accompanied by dogs while patrolling the crime-ridden streets. In Ghent, Belgium, in 1899, law enforcement began training dogs just for police duties. Dog breeding and training centers sprang up in Belgium, France, Austria-Hungary, and Germany. By the early 1900s, Germany was using K9 units in over 600 of their cities. German shepherds and Belgian Malinois were the main K9 breeds at this time, although Labrador retrievers and Dutch shepherds were also popular.

Police dogs in America in the 1900s

Starting in the early 1900s, several attempts were made by American law enforcement agencies to use police dogs. New York City began a K9 training center in 1910, which was modeled after the programs in Ghent, Belgium. In the 1940s and 1950s, other training and breeding programs sprang up in New Jersey, Maryland, Michigan, Oregon, and California.

In the 1970s, K9 training programs really took off in the United States as more police departments recognized that dependable K9 units made policing safer and easier. Today, police dogs are considered an essential part of most big-city police departments.

In 1912, a New York policeman holds several members of the forces's new K9 unit.

K9 HANDLERS

Handlers are the human half of K9 units. They are employed by police departments. Most get their start as regular patrol cops. K9 officers work about 40 hours per week, just like patrol cops. Handlers often refer to their dogs as "partners." Handlers are with their dogs 24 hours a day. They spend more time with their K9 partners than they do with their own families.

When K9s go home with their handlers, they are like pets. They are obedient and gentle with family members. Some even sleep in the same room as their handlers. When getting ready for work, handlers make sure their dogs are fed, are given any necessary veterinary medicines, and have the proper equipment needed for the workday.

Dutch shepherd Murphy and Officer Plum of Pennsylvania's Warrington Police K9 Unit, work, eat, and play together. On duty, the K9 team patrol and handle drug detection.

How to become a handler

To become handlers, police officers volunteer to be part of a K9 unit. If chosen, officers go through several hundred hours of school at special K9 training academies. They are paired with dogs that are good matches in personality. Officers learn about K9 behavior and the abilities dogs have when on patrol. Mostly, handlers and their dogs learn to work together as a team.

After 11 weeks of training, California Highway Patrol K9 handlers and their dogs graduate from a dual-purpose training course.

A K9 unit works a crime scene.

Shared stress

Being a K9 handler can be a stressful job. Because K9 units so often support other cops during dangerous situations, handlers usually see more action than regular patrol cops. On the other hand, it is reassuring for handlers to know their K9 partners are always there to help them. The dogs always have their backs. They will even give up their lives for their handlers without even thinking about it. Police dogs are there for their handlers during the best and the worst times. Many handlers say that the best part of their job is being able to work all day with their best friend.

BREEDS

Human police officers have special skills and abilities. Police K9s must also have certain skills. They need to be strong, obedient, and intelligent. They also require other special traits, depending on their jobs. K9s are bred to have the drive and mental toughness needed for police work.

Not all breeds are cut out to be good police dogs. Pomeranians and Yorkshire terriers make great companion animals but lousy K9 officers. There are a few special breeds that have the right instincts and skills to be trained police dogs. They must have a good sense of smell, be big enough to detain criminals, be aggressive, and fast. The most common K9 breeds today include Belgian Malinois, German shepherds, Dutch shepherds, bloodhounds, and Labrador retrievers.

Belgian Malinois are known for their speed and power.

Professional K9 trainers stand at attention with their dogs.

Costs and breeders

It is very expensive for police departments to maintain K9 units. The price for the dog alone can range from $5,000 to $10,000. Many dogs are imported from Europe, where strict breeding and training programs have existed for more than 100 years. American law enforcement often obtain their K9 units from dealers in Holland, Belgium, Germany, Slovakia, and the Czech Republic. There is also a growing network of breeders in the United States.

German shepherd

German shepherds are often the first dogs that come to mind when people think of police K9s. Important traits needed for any police dog are intelligence, sense of smell, aggression, and strength. German shepherds have all these traits in abundance. First bred in Germany, these dogs were originally used to herd farm animals such as sheep. They train well and are even tempered.

German shepherds are strong, athletic dogs with just the right mix of speed and stamina. They excel in attacking and apprehending criminals, biting down hard until the suspect is restrained, then letting go when their handlers command.

In addition to apprehending criminals, German shepherds are superb at using their noses to find hidden illegal items like drugs or explosives. They also track missing persons.

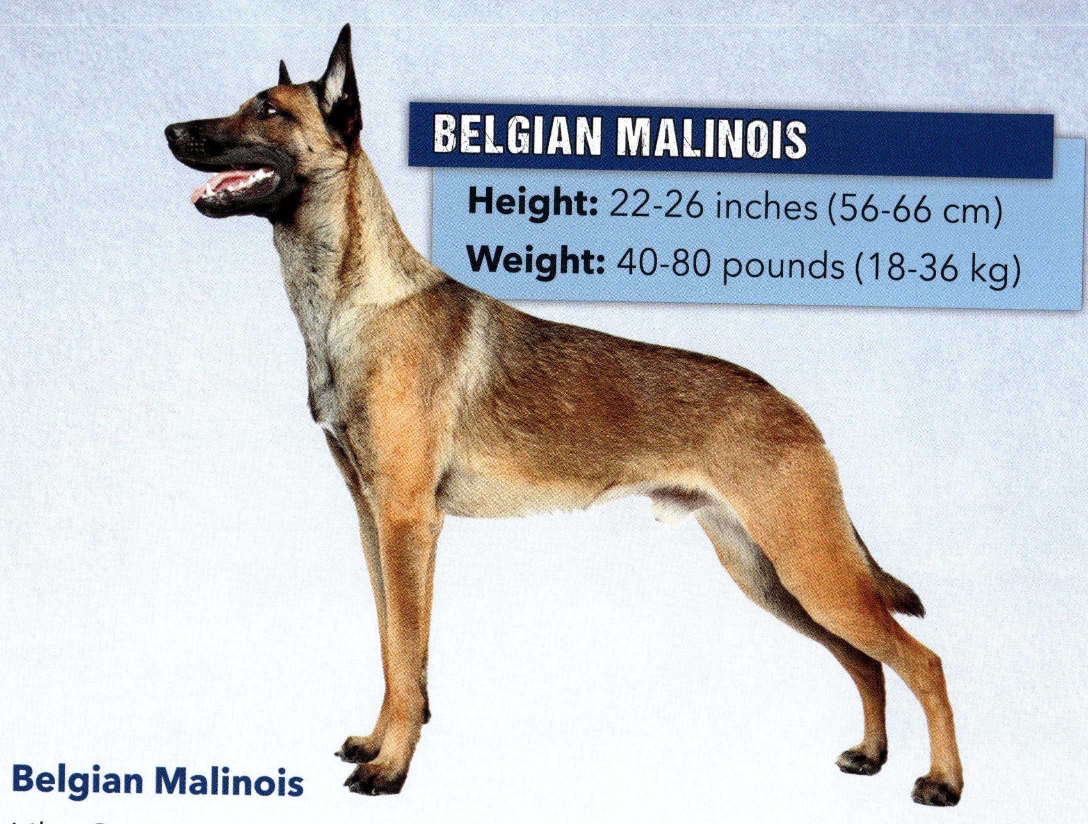

Belgian Malinois

Like German shepherds, Belgian Malinois (pronounced MAL-in-wah) were originally bred to be herding dogs. They are slightly lighter and faster than German shepherds. They are incredibly agile, able to run up sections of vertical surfaces, like brick and wooden walls, to gain access to second-story windows. They are alert, intelligent, and seemingly fearless. They are the preferred working dogs in many law enforcement agencies and United States military units today, including Navy SEALs.

The dogs get their name from Maline, Belgium, which is the town where they were first bred. They have a strong protection instinct and are loyal to their human handlers. In addition to apprehending criminals, they are excellent at finding hidden items or missing persons.

Dutch shepherd

Dutch shepherds are herding dogs, similar in appearance to German shepherds and Belgian Malinois. They were first found in the rural areas of the Netherlands, herding cows and sheep on farms. Intelligent and courageous, they were also good guard dogs, alerting farmers when strangers were nearby.

In the early 1900s, European law enforcement agencies began training Dutch shepherds for K9 duty. Today, they are valued for their intelligence, determination, and loyalty to their handlers. They are also obedient and eager to please.

Because of their physical strength and intelligence, Dutch shepherds make excellent dual-purpose K9 officers. They are strong enough to protect their handlers and detain criminals, and their noses are equipped to detect illegal narcotics or explosives.

Labrador retriever

Lovable Labrador retrievers are one of the most popular breeds in the United States. They also make great K9 officers. They are athletic, enthusiastic, and have an abundance of energy. Even though they are friendly with the public, labs aren't normally used as patrol dogs. However, their ultra-sensitive noses are great at detecting drugs, explosives, and other illegal items that may be hidden, including people. They are superior tracking dogs.

As search and rescue dogs, Labrador retrievers not only have their sensitive noses to aid them, they are also strong and agile. This helps them move around in odd, tight spaces, such as in the rubble of buildings after an earthquake or tornado.

Giant schnauzer

Giant schnauzers were first bred in today's Germany almost 400 years ago. They were used for many jobs around farms, including herding sheep and cattle. With their sturdy bodies and rough coats, they could easily withstand harsh winters and rugged mountain terrain. In the early 1900s, giant schnauzers were used as guard dogs. The German army also used them as war dogs during World War I and World War II. They became popular in the United States starting in the 1960s.

Today, giant schnauzers are used by law enforcement agencies for their superior sense of smell in detecting narcotics and explosives. Their muscular, imposing bodies also make them good patrol dogs. They obey commands well and can easily knock down and contain suspects to help their human handlers.

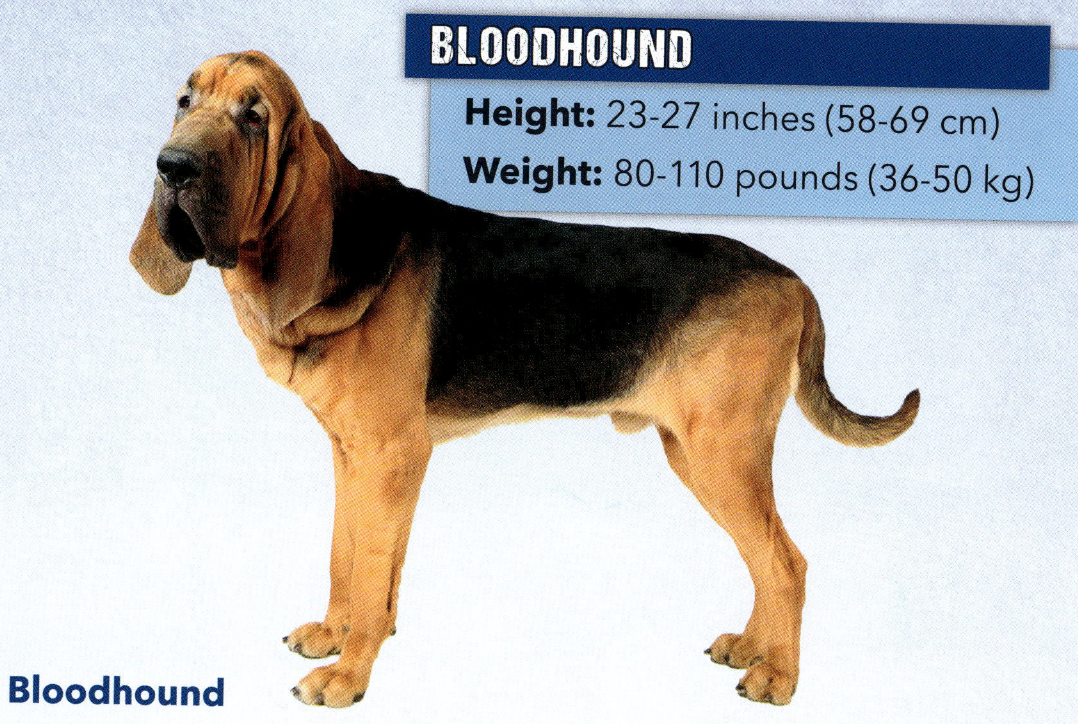

Bloodhound

For tracking escaped criminals or locating missing persons, it is hard to beat the sensitive nose of the bloodhound. These dogs have aided American cops since the late 1800s, but they have been in use all over the world for centuries. They are not patrol dogs, but they are superb at tracking even the faintest whiff of a missing person or criminal in hiding.

Bloodhounds have been bred specifically to track human beings. Their own slobber can rehydrate and enhance scents, and their large, floppy ears help waft odors to their noses. The "blood" in their name doesn't mean they are vicious. It simply means they have a high degree of breeding. In fact, bloodhounds are usually very gentle dogs.

Chapter 5

TRAINING AND EQUIPMENT

Dogs are almost always specially bred and trained at an early age to prepare them to become K9 officers. Not every dog is right for the job. They all have unique personalities, and this sometimes gets in the way of becoming a police dog. Some dogs are too easily distracted or lack the intelligence needed to become a K9 officer.

Obedience training

Police dogs must first pass rigorous obedience training. At first, young dogs are taught basic commands, such as "sit" and "stay." As training progresses, commands become more complex. They must obey all commands, even when it means setting aside their natural aggression. This is how human handlers control how much force K9 officers use when subduing a suspect.

Puppies who may become police dogs must be courageous in new situations and eager to please their handler.

A trainer and K9 have fun going through an obstacle course.

K9 academy

After human trainers volunteer for duty, they are sent to special K9 academies. Both trainer and dog are paired and go through training together. They work as a team. Training usually lasts 8 to 10 weeks. During K9 academy, the dogs and their assigned handlers get to know each other and learn to work together. After the academy, dogs and handlers train together for approximately a year before they're ready to go on patrol. Regular training continues for the rest of the dog's law enforcement career.

Police dogs need to be strong and nimble. Part of their training involves endurance and agility training. They learn to jump over walls, climbs stairs, and overcome many other obstacles.

Motivation

Handlers learn what best motivates their K9 partners, such as treats, toys, or even just praise. Police work is serious business, but dogs retain more information when training is kept light and fun.

Specialty training

The next step is specialty training. Many dogs learn to go on police patrol. They are trained very early on how to apprehend suspects. Some dogs learn to detect either drugs or explosives. Others become specialists in following scent trails in order to track criminals or missing persons.

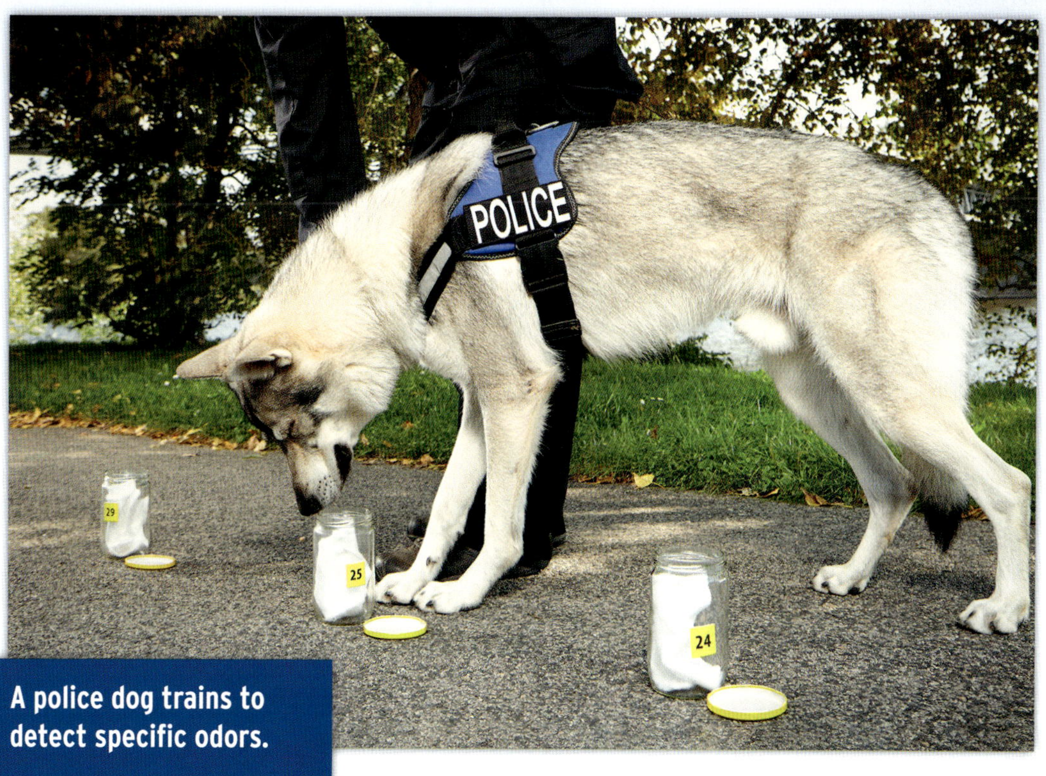

A police dog trains to detect specific odors.

Bite suits

When teaching K9 officers to take down and detain suspects, trainers wear specially padded bite suits. (Sometimes a simple bite sleeve is used.) Wearing a bite suit and getting clamped on by a K9 is like putting your arm in a vice. The dog bites down with enough pressure to sometimes bruise. The K9 will not let go until called off by its handler. To actually get bit is very painful. Police K9s bite deeply into the flesh, and they keep chomping the more a suspect resists.

Muzzles

Muzzles are used in training and as a safety tool while on patrol. There are several styles, from wire cages to lightweight fabric mesh. Muzzles keep dogs from opening their mouths wide so they don't accidentally bite someone, but there is enough room to pant and lick their noses.

FOREIGN LANGUAGE COMMANDS

People may notice that many police dogs in the United States respond only to commands in a foreign language, such as German or Dutch. It is a myth that the dogs are taught this way so that a criminal cannot tell a dog to attack in English. In reality, young dogs are trained with command words in their native language. When they arrive in the United States, it is easier for their human handlers to learn a few commands in German or Dutch than it is to retrain the dogs in English.

Harnesses

Almost all police dogs wear a collar and some sort of harness. Many harnesses, also called tactical vests, have a handle on top so the dog can be restrained, or more easily lifted over tall obstacles. Harnesses often have a badge identifying the K9 officer. In addition to harnesses, some dogs wear padded traction booties on their paws if they are being sent into areas where there may be sharp objects.

Protective vests

Some dogs that regularly encounter violent criminals, such as those that are sent on search warrant duty, are outfitted with bullet- and stab-resistant vests. They are made of the same dense Kevlar fabric that human bullet-resistant vests are made from. Although they protect K9 officers from possible harm, the vests are heavy, hot, and constrictive. Protective vests are very expensive. Sometimes communities chip in to help pay for their police departments' K9 vests.

To protect police dogs, some K9 cruisers are equipped with temperature monitoring systems that alert the handlers when the interior of the vehicles reach a specific heat level.

Patrol car accessories

When riding in a squad car with their human partners, K9 officers ride in the back seat. A special metal barrier separates dogs from people riding in front. Dog crates are also sometimes used. The most important thing is that the K9 officer be provided with plenty of water and ventilation, especially on hot summer days.

Some K9 patrol cars are equipped with remote door openers. If a human partner is outside the vehicle and needs emergency help, the cop can flip a switch on his or her belt to remotely pop open the back door. This allows K9 officers to leap out and assist.

Chapter 6

K9 OFFICERS ON THE JOB

Police departments in large cities often use different breeds of dogs for different jobs. Many dogs, however, are trained to perform more than one duty. For example, the Miami, Florida, police department has a K9 unit with German shepherds and Belgian Malinois. They are all trained to track and catch criminals who are running and hiding. After 480 hours of training to track and apprehend, the dogs then learn how to use their noses to sniff and find hidden drugs or explosives.

Apprehension

The most important use of a K9 patrol dog is to detain dangerous criminals until they are put in handcuffs. Sometimes just the sight of a police dog or the sound of its furious bark is enough to make criminals surrender without a fight. Handlers take advantage of the dogs' instinct to chase prey. K9 "fur missiles" can catch up to fleeing suspects in seconds and knock them off their feet. They bite down on a limb and stubbornly hold on until human cops arrive to make an arrest. K9 officers are trained to bite only on the command of their human partners and must release when told to do so.

K9 officers are trained to detain suspected criminals.

A Massachusetts State Police K9 presses his nose against a car door when he finds hidden drugs.

Detection

Dogs have many more scent receptors in their nasal cavities than humans, who only have about 6 million. By contrast, bloodhounds have an astounding 300 million scent receptors, allowing the search and rescue dogs to follow scent trails for many miles. Dogs are also aware of a "fear scent." That is the sweat and adrenaline given off by suspects being tracked and chased.

Although tracking criminals is an important K9 job, the majority of their detection work is spent sniffing for hidden contraband. Some dogs specialize in drugs or explosives, but never both.

During a vehicle stop, if a police officer suspects the occupants may have drugs hidden inside the car, the cop may call for a K9 unit. The dog is allowed by law to sniff around the vehicle. If the K9 detects the odor of illegal drugs inside, it "alerts," usually by lying down or pressing its face against the car. The cops are then allowed to search the vehicle and arrest the occupants if drugs or other illegal items are discovered.

SCENT TRAINING

Dogs love new smells and can be trained to sniff out almost anything, including drugs, chemicals, explosives, dead bodies, diseases, and even bed bugs! To train K9 officers to locate scents, trainers use a play and reward system. A favorite toy is laced with a scent. The trainer plays games like hide-and-seek with the dog, which receives praise and a reward when the toy is discovered. Eventually, the toy is replaced with real drugs or other objects the dog is being trained to find. When the dog finds the item, it lies down next to it in order to alert the handler, who then rewards the dog with its favorite toy.

A K9 performs an article search in a wooded area.

Article searches

Article searches are used to find missing pieces of evidence from crime scenes. When suspects flee from police, they sometimes discard illegal items that will get them into more trouble. K9 units are called to the scene to find the evidence, which might include firearms or narcotics. Article searches can take place in a building, in the woods, a field, or even a parking lot.

When a dog is on an article sweep, it can cover an area quickly. It would take a human cop more than 10 times as long to search the same amount of ground as a K9, and the officer would probably miss many things a dog's sensitive nose detects.

Dogs trained for article searches can be highly specialized. The Miami, Florida, K9 unit has a dog with the sole job of sniffing out hidden money. Another dog specializes in finding guns and spent bullet casings that litter the ground after a shooting. Some dogs are trained to detect dead bodies that have been buried.

K9 Jax of Minnesota's
Eden Prairie Police
Department sits by
the drugs and money
he uncovered during a
traffic stop.

Search and rescue

When a crime victim is kidnapped, a child gets lost in the woods, or a natural disaster causes buildings to collapse, law enforcement officials call out for search and rescue teams. In many cases, K9 officers join in the hunt. Some dogs are specifically trained to find human scents, whether the victims are alive or dead. Bloodhounds are especially good at performing search and rescue, although German shepherds, Belgian Malinois, and Labrador retrievers are also commonly used.

Dogs can lock onto the scent of a single individual. They can track somebody by keeping their noses to the ground, which is called tracking. Trailing is when the dogs also sniff the air. This allows them to detect scent cones that waft in the breeze. The narrower and more concentrated the cone, the closer the dog is to the victim.

Smart and brave

Search and rescue K9 officers are extremely hard working. Their intelligence and concentration allow them to ignore the scents of other people and focus on the missing person. They can search wide areas in a very short time, with high accuracy. They are also able to enter hazardous places, such as collapsed buildings, that are dangerous for human searchers. They can even find people who have been buried in avalanches, or drowning victims who are submerged underwater.

A German shepherd on a training exercise digs to find a victim buried in snow.

Chapter 7

A POLICE DOG'S LIFE

Police dogs live with their human partners. In many cases, they have an outside kennel, but oftentimes the dogs live inside with their handlers and their families. Many dogs are gentle family pets, but when it's time to go to work, K9 officers are all business.

Many K9 handlers pay for some food and veterinarian expenses out of their own pockets. Unlike most family pets, police dogs are very high-energy animals. The food they eat is a special formula that gives them the nutrition they need.

A typical workday for a K9 officer may start with a drug sweep at a school or business. This might be followed by a trip to court, where the handler testifies against a suspect, or defends against a claim that excessive force was used in an arrest. A dog's training record is important in such claims.

During an eight-hour patrol shift, a K9 unit goes on a variety of calls. These range from assisting in arrests to tracking burglary suspects. K9 units are usually kept busy throughout the shift.

Police dogs normally retire when they are about 10 years old. Senior dogs cannot withstand the rigors and stress of police work. When K9 officers retire, they are usually adopted by their handlers and go to live with their families.

Inga, a decorated bloodhound with California's Riverside County Sheriff's Department, worked for more than nine years before retiring to live in the country with her partner, Deputy Garvin.

PUBLIC DEMONSTRATIONS

Police dogs are some of the best public relations tools that cops have available to them. Police call it "community engagement." Many K9 units do demonstrations with public groups, such as schools and community gatherings. It's a way for the public to see what the dogs can do to combat crime, and how they help police and the community. It's also a way for the police to connect with the community and to show how they do their jobs. They use the dogs as a tool to come together with the people they serve.

A police demonstration of a K9 "fur missile" shows how it can take down a criminal.

Furry goodwill ambassadors

Most people respond positively to the dogs, especially kids and young adults. K9 partners give police officers extra opportunities to build goodwill and be part of the community.

The police can then use their ties with citizens to solve crimes and assist with other issues that affect neighborhoods. Thanks to K9 patrols, these new partnerships help make cities and towns better places to live.

K9 Dusty and his partner Officer Rob Korth meet kids at a Wisconsin school. Dusty works as a scent dog.

GLOSSARY

arrest – When a person suspected of committing a crime is taken into custody by a law enforcement officer.

breed – A group of animals within a species that have a similar appearance. A German shepherd and a bloodhound are from the same species, but are different breeds. There are approximately 340 dog breeds worldwide.

contraband – Goods such as narcotics or explosives that are illegal to own, possess, or smuggle into a place.

detain – When a police officer stops a person for brief questioning, possibly before a formal arrest.

fugitive – Someone who has escaped from, or is in hiding from, law enforcement personnel, usually in order to avoid being arrested for committing a crime.

Kevlar – A light and strong man-made fiber. It is used to make bullet-resistant vests, helmets, and other protective gear for law enforcement and military personnel.

narcotics – Drugs such as LSD or heroin that are illegal to possess or use.

scent cone – An imaginary cone-shaped area in the air. It begins from the source of a scent, such as a person, drugs, or explosives, and spreads out downwind. The cone widens as it gets farther from the source. K9 trackers move back and forth across the cone. As the scent gets more concentrated, the dog knows it is getting closer and closer to the source.

suspect – Someone suspected of committing a crime.

warrant – An arrest warrant authorizes the police to arrest someone suspected of committing a crime. A search warrant allows the search of a person, vehicle, or building.

ONLINE RESOURCES

To learn more about K9s, visit abdobooklinks.com or scan this QR code. These links are routinely monitored and updated to provide the most current information available.

INDEX